My 1st Classic Story

The Shoemaker and His Elves

a retelling of the Grimm's fairy tale

by Eric Blair

illustrated by Bill Dickson

PICTURE WINDOW BOOKS
a capstone imprint

My First Classic Story is published by Picture Window Books
A Capstone Imprint
151 Good Counsel Drive, P.O. Box 669
Mankato, Minnesota 56002
www.capstonepub.com

Originally published by Picture Window Books, 2004.
Copyright © 2011 by Picture Window Books.

Printed in the United States of America in North Mankato, Minnesota.
032010
005740CGF10

Library of Congress Cataloging-in-Publication Data
Blair, Eric.
The shoemaker and his elves : a retelling of the Grimms' fairy
tale / retold by Eric Blair ; illustrated by Bill Dickson.
p. cm. — (My first classic story)
Summary: An easy-to-read retelling of the classic tale of a kindly
but poor shoemaker who gets unexpected help with his work.
ISBN 978-1-4048-6077-3 (library binding)
[1. Fairy tales. 2. Folklore—Germany.] I. Dickson, Bill, ill.
II. Grimm, Jacob, 1785-1863. III. Grimm, Wilhelm, 1786-1859.
IV. Elves and the shoemaker. English. V. Title.
PZ8.B5688Sh 2011
398.2—dc22
[E]   2010003628

Art Director: Kay Fraser
Graphic Designer: Emily Harris

The story of *The Shoemaker and His Elves* has been passed down for generations. There are many versions of the story. The following tale is a retelling of the original version. While the story has been cut for length and level, the basic elements of the classic tale remain.

There once was a poor shoemaker. He could buy only enough leather to make one pair of shoes at a time.

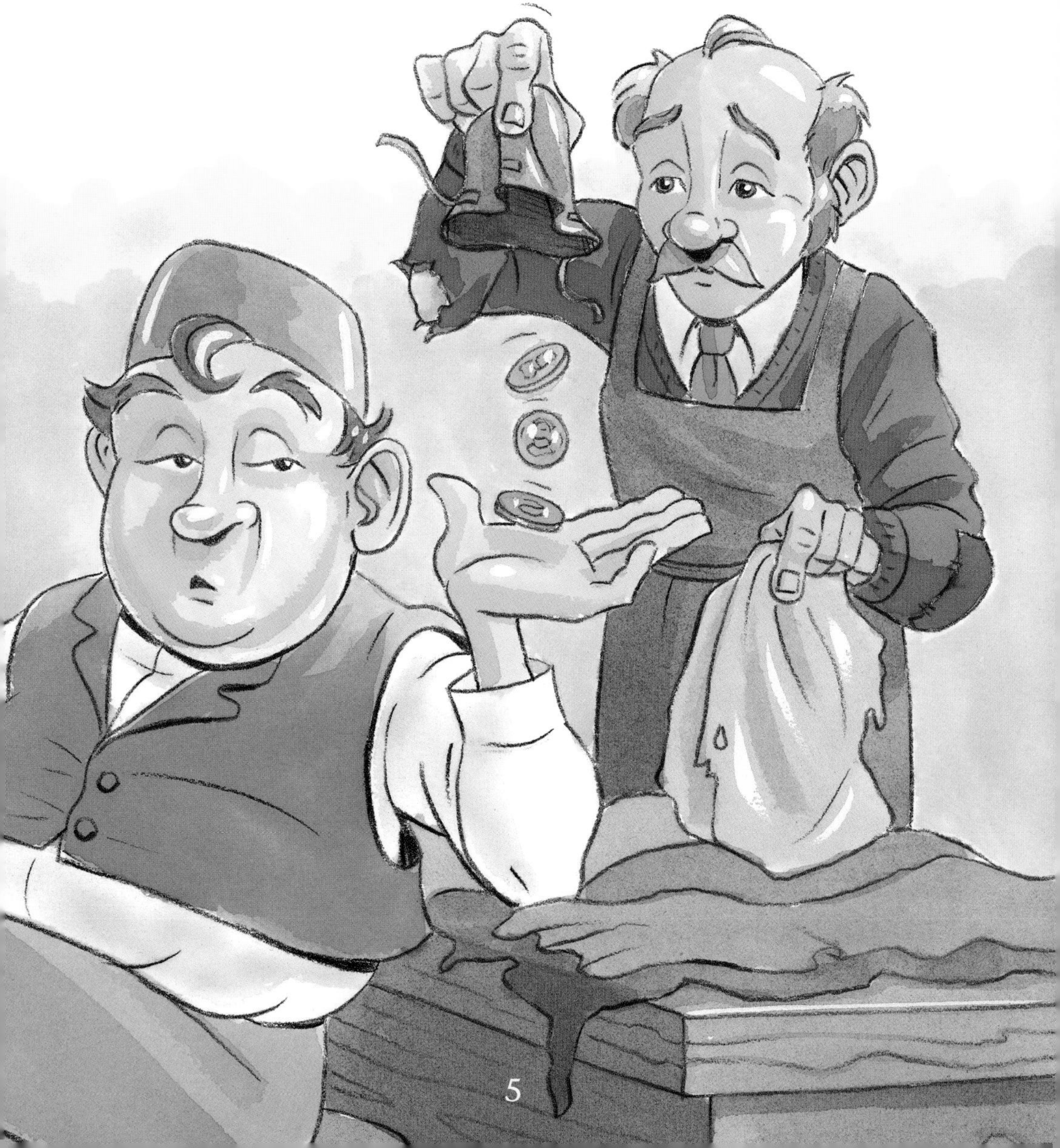

One night, he cut the leather for the
shoes he wanted to make the next day.
Then he went to bed.

The next morning, a pair of shoes was already made! The shoes were perfect.

A rich man paid twice the price for them.
The shoemaker was able to buy enough
leather for two pairs of shoes.

Again he cut the leather for the shoes he planned to make the next day.

The next morning, two pairs of shoes were made. These shoes sold right away, too. The shoemaker made enough money to buy leather for four pairs of shoes.

The next morning, four pairs of shoes
were made. And so it went.

The shoemaker made a lot of money.
Before long, he was rich.

One night, he said to his wife, "Let's stay up tonight. Maybe we can see who is helping us."

That night, the shoemaker and his wife hid.

Around midnight, two naked little men sat down at the table. They worked all night.

The shoemaker and his wife watched.

When the shoes were done, the little
men ran away.

"Those two little men have made us rich.
We should help them," the wife said.

"What should we do?" asked the shoemaker.

"Well, they don't have any clothes," his wife said. "I will make them shirts, coats, pants, and socks."

"And I will make them shoes," the shoemaker said.

The shoemaker and his wife waited for Christmas Eve. Then they put the shoes and the clothes on the table.

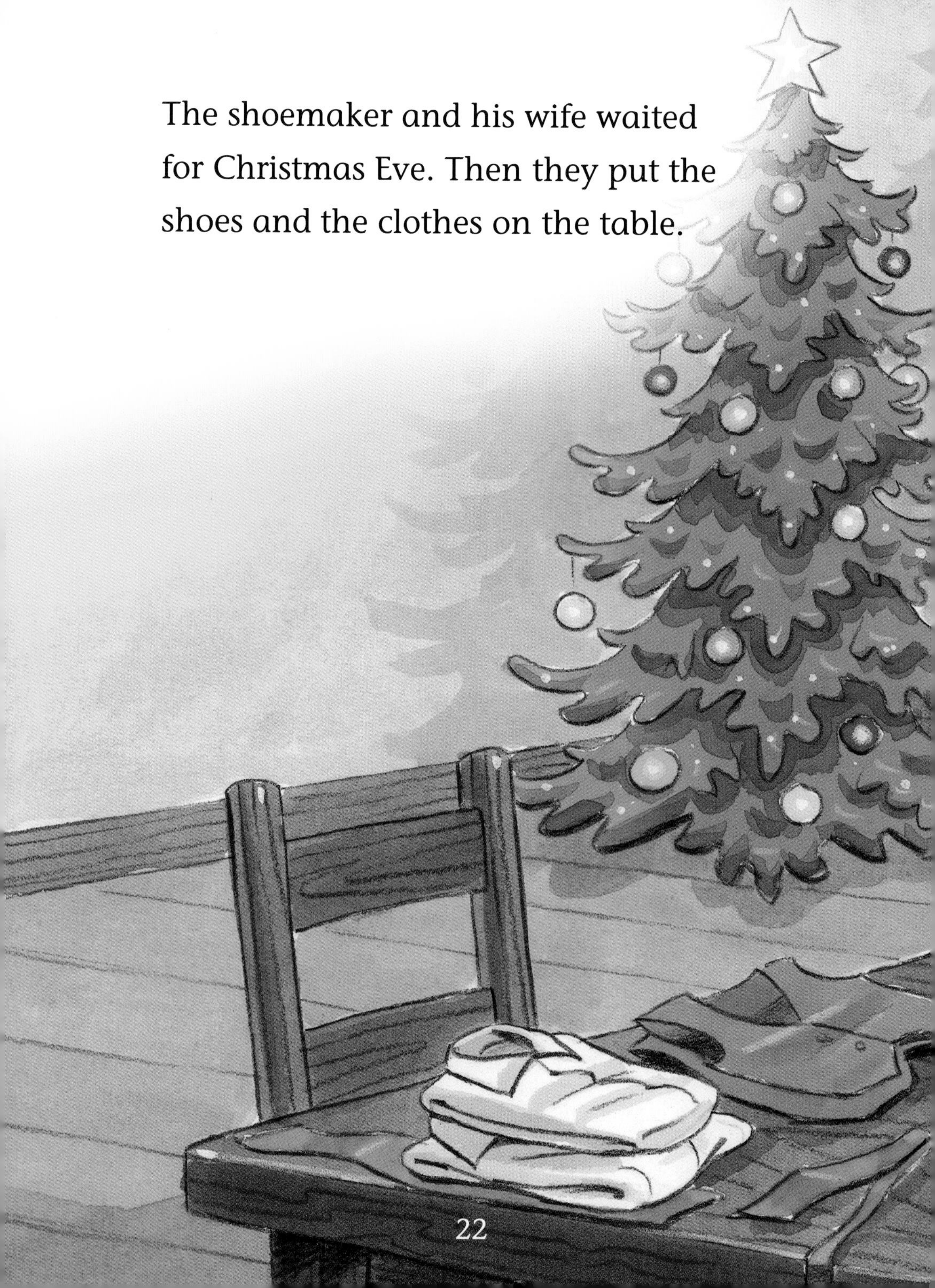

Around midnight, the little men showed up again.

They saw the shoes and the clothes.

They were very surprised.

They quickly put the clothes on.
Then they started to sing.

26

"Now we are men so fine to see," they sang.
"No longer shoemakers shall we be."

The little men danced and danced.

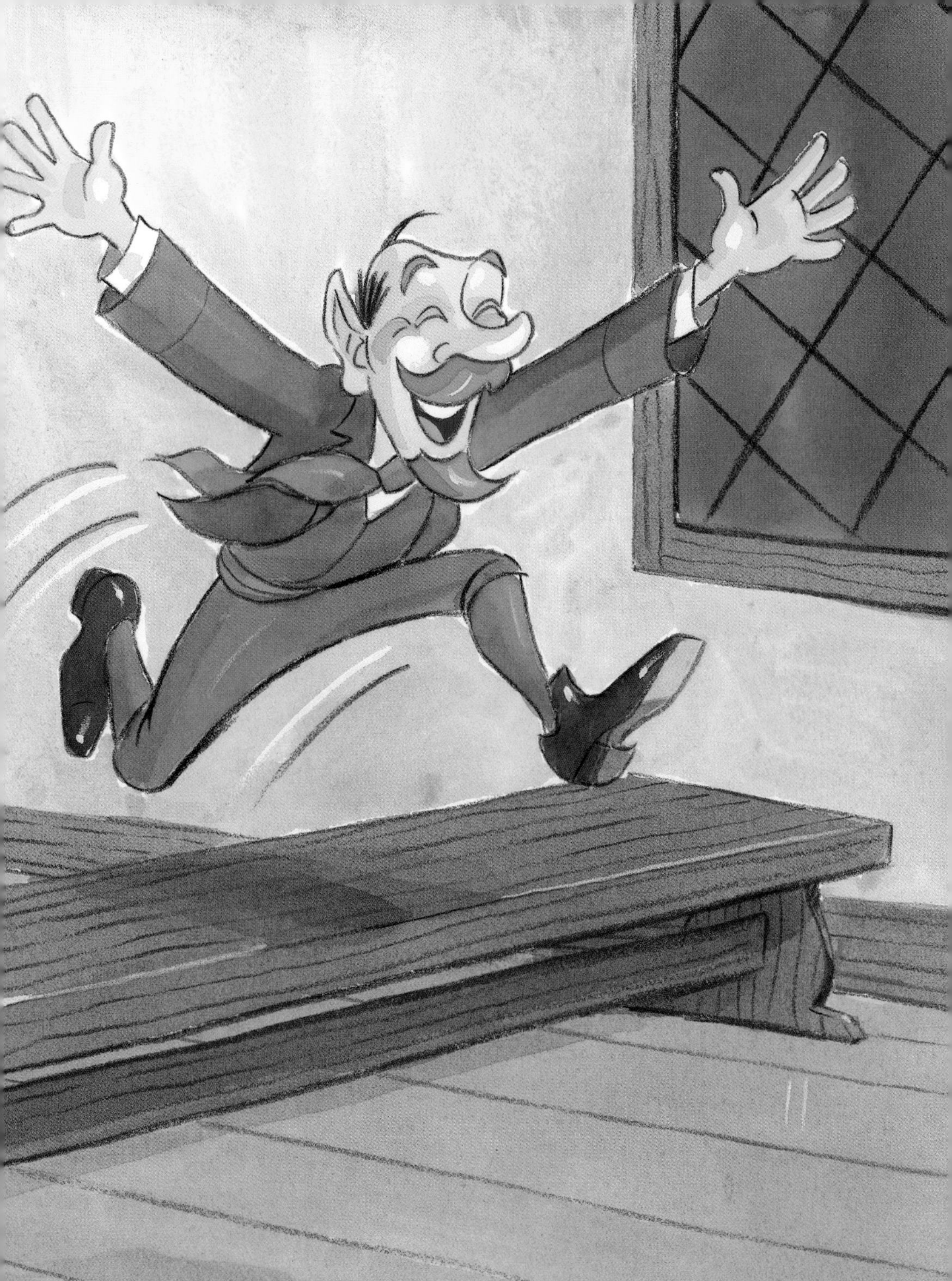

At last, they danced out the door.
They were never seen again.

The shoemaker and his wife were rewarded for their good deeds. They succeeded in everything they tried. And they lived happily ever after.

The End